We Speak of Flowers

Eileen Chong is an Australian poet who was born in Singapore of Hakka, Hokkien and Peranakan descent. She is the author of ten books published in Australia and the United States. Major prizes her work has been shortlisted for include the NSW Premier's Literary Award, the Victorian Premier's Literary Award, and twice for the Prime Minister's Literary Award. Her debut book, *Burning Rice*, is the first poetry collection by an Asian Australian to be studied as part of the NSW HSC English syllabus. Her most recent collection with UQP, *A Thousand Crimson Blooms*, was shortlisted for the Kenneth Slessor Prize for Poetry. She lives and works on the unceded land of the Gadigal of the Eora Nation. eileenchong.com.au

We Speak of Flowers

EILEEN CHONG

UQP

First published 2025 by University of Queensland Press
PO Box 6042, St Lucia, Queensland 4067 Australia

University of Queensland Press (UQP) acknowledges the Traditional Owners and
their custodianship of the lands on which UQP operates. We pay our respects to their
Ancestors and their descendants, who continue cultural and spiritual connections to
Country. We recognise their valuable contributions to Australian and global society.

uqp.com.au
reception@uqp.com.au

Cover design by Madeline Byrne, University of Queensland Press
Cover artwork by Heman Chong
Author photograph by Travis De Vries
Typeset in 11.5/14 pt Adobe Garamond Pro by Post Pre-press Group, Brisbane
Printed in Australia by McPherson's Printing Group

 University of Queensland Press is supported by the
Queensland Government through Arts Queensland.

  This project has been assisted by the
Australian Government through Creative
Australia, its principal arts investment and
advisory body.

 This project is supported by the NSW Government through Create NSW.

A catalogue record for this book is available from the National Library of Australia.

ISBN 978 0 7022 6862 5 (pbk)
ISBN 978 0 7022 6988 2 (epdf)

University of Queensland Press uses papers that are natural, renewable and recyclable
products made from wood grown in well-managed forests and other controlled sources.
The logging and manufacturing processes conform to the environmental regulations of
the country of origin.

A poem for my ancestors

How, then, may I
speak of flowers
here, where
a world of forms convulses

Li-Young Lee

To be a Flower, is profound
Responsibility –

Emily Dickinson

Author's Note

We Speak of Flowers is a book-length poem in 101 fragments that can be read in any order. Each reading will construct the poem anew, and the shifting juxtapositions will give rise to innumerable permutations of the poem.

The inspiration for this structure came from my Hakka, Hokkien and Peranakan ancestors' religious and cultural practices, particularly around the processes of grieving and death. In Buddhist belief, after a person has died, the soul exists in a liminal space for the first forty-nine days, before it is finally reborn after a total of 100 days. This marks the end of the formal process of grieving the dead.

Each fragment, then, is a meditation on mourning, with the final fragment marking the moment of the soul's reincarnation on the wheel of life (samsara), or its release from samsara (thus attaining nirvana). An end is also a beginning.

It is my hope that this book can be a companion to you for as long as you wish, and that each reading of the poem reconnects you to your own processes of grieving and healing. The beauty of a flower, and of life, lies precisely in its transience.

Eileen Chong

1

a singular, cracked voice

words matter, can still rise—

2

I want to be honest in this poem, which is not the same
thing as being truthful. I will speak of what happened,
of what could have happened, and of what continues to
happen: to you, to me, to them, to us. I will use what tools
I have, what the page will hold. What passes for words.
What words pass us.

3

You laugh at my speech.
Even my name is wrong.
My tongue will not bend;
I cannot read these titles.
I do not speak these words.

4

I wake myself in the dark, talking.
I stand in the garden and face the sea.
The north wind tugs at the wet
fabric in my hands. I fasten it:
the shirt a trapped white flag.

5

If an ancestor had continued south,
what then? A market garden, goldfields,
a laundry, the family restaurant? Not this
bloodless mining of words, this stymied pen.

6

Write for your people, they tell me.

My people of the river delta.
My people of the crossed seas.

Northern people who became
Southern people. *No people—*

My people who lost their language.
Who carved out new worlds.

Grandfathers of grandfathers:
illegible words in a ledger.

The order of misspelled names
written wrongly on all the forms.

I call these names in the night.
My people, I cry. *My people—*

There is no answer.
They are long cold in the earth.

They are far beyond communion.

7

This was no funeral like my grandfather's.
Nothing went up in smoke except for her body.

No blankets embroidered with Chinese
characters hung up like before. Even

the crematorium had a face lift—the soft
glow of lamps, the inside cavernous with pews.

At the front, no cross or altar: just space, and the furnace.

A family on a boat. Ashes in a bright
red bundle. Prayers, a Buddhist monk,

his rung bell. The hour her remains were released
into the sea, we were in the ocean, the water

sucking at our feet. We looked beyond to the horizon.
All bodies of water are connected, I lied. *She is with us now.*

Her hand cold in mine as she cried for her mother.

8

A magpie one day, a currawong the next.
Cockatoos screamed and wheeled away.

Which bird was her spirit made manifest?
No song I heard turned into dream.

The cuckoo in the red clock nodded to the hours.

We arrived in the rain, and drove for miles
away from the city. Outside the cemetery gates

we gathered handfuls of wild daisies. The sun
burned in the thin sky. Headstones like giant

fingertips thrust from beneath the earth.
He stopped: *my grandparents*—I bent to place

the flowers at their graves, and pulled at the weeds.
Nettles stung me, and I cried out in pain.

He nodded. *It's Tommy and Senga, saying they see you.*

9

A single mahjong tile: mouth shot through
with a spear; a globe spinning on its axis.

Her kitchen in my kitchen; her hands ghostly
on mine. We feed the ones we love. We scrape

our bowls clean. We scrub them white as bone.

What does it mean for a life
when you know you will be no-one's ancestor?

Hungry every waking minute. We count
the ribs of prisoners of war. Bloodlines

blurred like ink on crumpled, clutched tickets.

10

Someday a girl will read this and think
of survival. Another girl once scaled

a mud wall and escaped into the night,
carrying only two pilfered buns

and a fragment of jade from her mother.
She did not know where she would end up.

She began in darkness so I might become light.

11

Another summer. Insects thrum
and the leaves are heavy with salt.

Nothing has changed. Everything
is different. The sea water in the pool

has come and gone a thousand times
since we last swam here together.

The grass, the rocks, the sea floor:
they remain. The crabs in the crevices,

the clinging limpets. You will not remember
this. You are beyond all remembering.

I submerge myself in the ocean.
My body knows you were once here.

The tide comes in and breaks on the chains.

12

In my dreams, I return to the staircase. I hurry down the steps. They are wide and wooden, then narrow and metal, and wind through people's homes, through rooms crammed full of their lives. My mission is to descend without being seen, stopped, caught. I do not know why I run, or what I run from. I wake up tired, and ascend another stair.

13

I have dreamed about
your death for as long

as I have drawn breath. When
a lizard fell from the lintel into

my palms, eyes dark
in its translucent head.

When the road diverged—
cars and buses ploughing

past, and a small figure
was dragged, bloodying.

The shins of the trishaw rider:
bones stark through leathered skin.

14

Boiled sweets in our mouths
dissolved into shards and sliced

our tongues into a thousand forks.
Even the numbers would not lie

at rest. Jade rounds slipped
from shrunken wrists, fell

and smashed upon landing. Bury
the pieces on a hill in salt, or in a grave

when the moon no longer watches.
It will be my turn to embark on

the silent, unknown journey. The dawn
will break like a bright black bird.

15

What is the use of a full moon
now we do not harvest by its light?

There is no-one else standing here,
lifting their face to the star-studded sky.

Do you see the moon's craters, its dark side?
It simply hangs there, brilliant white—

In the living room the children
and I mime spinning on an axis.

We tread an elliptical path around
the sun of the dying woman. Later,

she gifts me six pieces of gold.
Weight of a blessing from the living:

a Möbius bangle, blue sapphires in bezels.
Her name in Arabic, hanging from a chain.

16

Almásy said, *Every night I cut out my heart*
but in the morning it was full again.

Black consumes the luminous orb,
even as the girl learns how to spell

gibbous, waxing, waning. Do not swallow
the bright coin we place under your tongue—

A bolus of bread. It rises,
it fills with air, it is eaten.

Dust to flesh to dust to dust.
The frozen smiles of family

framed in silver. I draw the curtains.
Moonlight falls across the bed linen.

Behind your lids, all will fade, and turn to ink.
Outside, a curlew cries. We see the glitter of a scythe.

17

I was a child who was often laughed at for crying. I cried at many things: at the thunderstorms that raged outside and within, at silence and neglect, at the loneliness that would never leave me. They stood me in the corner, facing the walls. Once, I was carried to an empty bathtub and placed within it so I could fill it with my tears. Release the plug. Let my grief disappear down the drain, into the nameless sea.

18

the paintings we bought   of the interior
of someone else's   home now come across

as somewhat ironic   such black and white
it seems   do we know when to unmask

ourselves   how far should we stand
from those we love   gloves make

for poor intimacy   I caught sight
of a man at his desk   by a window previously

always shuttered   he saw me sweating
on my exercise machine   dressed in only a chemise

I was ashamed

I heard the music next door   and thought
of our ex-neighbour who loved   spanking

we would listen through the walls   and wonder
who was hurting the most   there are people

sitting on park benches   their eyes follow me
I worry   they can tell I am Asian underneath

ticker tongues send out   numbers in the thousands
sites crash and burn   your colleague

has curious taste in art   she gets up
sits inside the closet   I feel lucky

I am childless   dream about jars and wake to
measure   rise not descend write it down

the sun is watery   we have missed the summer
do leaves even fall   if you are no longer a witness

19

The lines stretch out like a child's drawing,
wavering, circling the block. These are people,
they clutch at bags, papers, proof of lack.

They are hungry; they are afraid of going hungry.
What price is dignity? A reporter says *No*, she will not
go to the front of the line to demand answers.

The cafes are shuttered. There are no rooms
to while away the hours of the night, drinking.
A bed so narrow it barely contains

a single body lying flat on its back.
Sheets pulled back like a discarded shroud.
Behind the façade whole alphabets are set loose.

Imagine the touch of a stranger—an unknown gift,
a leap of faith. A breath and its attendant dangers.
The carpet glitters with piles of spilled-over numbers.

20

In the scintillating blue
I'm behind you   Look up:
foam crest, surge and pull

The wave rears up, frozen
like in the woodblock print
I wake : before we both drown

        What did she see in the bath
        mirrored feet turned backwards
        stumps rising   between buildings

Restless spirits left to wander
follow roundabout prints in the mud
You run from / towards the past

Stilts will not save us
Here was our home : now encircled
by tangled salt water

In the last kingdom before the tide
we make cups of bitter tea
grey water sucking at our ankles

21

the afternoon heat nearly unbearable
we spill forth, naked, towards the water
cautiously picking our way to avoid

submerged rocks and broken branches
read the current, you call out
I am tired of reading everything

three cormorants perch on the riverbend
wet wings open to the wind
bird poems flood in without invitation

later, I open tins of food by the fire
we lie under wide, dark skies
the stars overhead pencilled in and labelled

verses follow one another
into opaque documents over the years
books left on the grass, sodden with rain

22

From before memory, I remember. Memory finds its locus in my body. I undress, I wash, I dress. In the mirror my body shimmers when I tilt my head from left to right, right to left. Memory's eyes do not leave me. Or perhaps it is my eyes that do not leave it. I used to pray every night for four angels to guard the corners of my bed. I worried that they had the names of men.

23

I close my eyes and I'm four again—
we're at the crossing, waiting for the light.
Your hand around mine. You carried
a bag of eggs: ten, I'd counted. You showed
me how to crack the shells, taught me how
to beat the eggs and mix them with stock.
I watched you pour the pale liquid into a dish
and lower it into the lidded wok. I love steamed
egg custard: its soft simplicity, its gentle savour.

24

I lay with you that final time in your big bed.
I don't remember what we were watching on TV.
I recall the curtains, and how I'd asked you
to sew me dresses from that same fabric.
You laughed, and offered me your red lace dress.
I didn't take it. I wish I had now.
They didn't dress you in it, but placed it in your coffin.
It burned, like everything else, to ash.
I wish I'd been there. I would have worn it.

25

I deleted your number from my phone.
I'll never forget it, or you. Some days
I hear your voice, talking about everything
and nothing. I miss your curses, your loud,
careless laugh. I even miss your driving.
I only drove you once. You didn't criticise
my parking. Remember the restaurant in the old theatre?
They'd served us buns in the shape of peaches.
I close my eyes, still taste them.

26

Sifting through the remnants of what was left unsold,
my mother uncovers three steel cooking implements:

two ladles (one larger, the other shallower) and a wide,
splayed spatula. Their bodies are burnished gunmetal;

their wooden handles have been worn smooth.
They gleam with the patina of heat and daily use.

There is but a single photograph of our hawker stall.
My grandfather, his dark hair raked back, poses

in the foreground. Spoons laden with sambal and narrow wedges
of lime line the front counter. Yellow and white noodles nest

behind glass, next to eggs stacked high on cardboard trays.
The immense wok; the roaring flame. Plumes of smoke—

Where is my grandmother? The tools of her trade now lie
unmoving in a box. Her smile grows still in a shadowed frame.

27

Once, in her kitchen, her grandchildren crowded around
the stove, watching. No-one had thought to take notes.

She minced garlic with a cleaver and, in one smooth
movement, scooped and tossed its contents into scalding oil.

How the garlic would sizzle. The aroma of its browning.
Eggs cracked and beaten in the pan, handfuls of noodles

eased from a tangled mass. Shelled prawns (heads and tails
left on) and a ladled measure of stock. She scraped at iron

with the spatula, crisping the ingredients, mixing them in, then
rapped hard, thrice, on the edge of the wok. Sparks would fly.

Next, the plates: each piled with steaming fried prawn noodles
thick with gravy, complex with spice, and sharpened by citrus.

No record but in these tools. This hunger: my only inheritance.
I raise my chopsticks, lift the noodles to my lips, and I feast.

28

Peking opera heard
through a door, faintly—

       I raise my eyes from the page:
    it is a child who is only myself.

We pull on clothes and shoes,
rub our knuckles raw.

    Count out the coins collected
        for the night's lottery.

You hang the washing on lines crisscrossing
the landing. *He told you not to smoke up here!*

29

They are at it again:
another baby in the new year.

Ashes of wood, ashes of paper.
Poison heaped in bowls like rice.

No-one believes anyone anymore,
even when it is the whole truth.

Footsteps on the stairs,
singing down the corridor.

I return my eyes to books:
words like worms, eating everything.

30

Lonely, I turn on the TV for some company
while I fold joss paper in the shape of ingots.
My grandmother must have run out of them
by now, three years on from her death.

While I fold joss paper in the shape of ingots,
I watch the on-screen family eat dinner together.
By now, three years on from her death,
I should have stopped mourning my grandmother.

I watch the on-screen family eat dinner together.
They don't talk. Daughter serves food to father.
I should have stopped mourning my grandmother,
but here I am, folding ingots from joss paper.

They don't talk. Daughter serves food to father;
the father accepts her gesture without words.

Here, I am folding ingots from joss paper.
My hands are tired but the pile is growing.

The father accepts her gesture without words.
We know this is devotion. This is unspoken love.
My hands are tired but the pile is growing.
I will light some incense and burn these offerings.

We know this is devotion. This is unspoken love.
She is dead. There is nothing more to say.
I light some incense and burn these offerings.
They will pass from this world to the other.

She is dead. There is nothing more to say.
I dream of her, then wake and remember
she has passed from this world to the other.
Alone, I turn up the TV. Ghosts are too-silent company.

31

My lover fingers my scars. He counts them, seam by seam.
There are others he does not see; here are wounds not yet
grown over. He says my scars are the remnants of the mould
I was punched out from. Memories, histories, pathways.
Some days I wake up and forget what bed, which country,
whose body I inhabit.

32

In the evening we walk past
the ruined castle towards the loch.

The sun is setting behind us.
There is a walled garden full

of rose bushes without a single
bloom. It's too late in the season.

I read about the receding waters
of Lake Mead, and how the remains

of bodies began to surface. Did they
fall? Jump? Were they thrown? Sunk?

When I first learned how to swim,
my brother would dive underwater

and close a hand around my ankle.
My panicked kicking did the rest.

If a ghost catches you, they will
take your body. You'll trade places.

If I'm not careful, I'll remember
what it feels like to float, unanchored.

We stand by the bank as the light fails,
as the swans turn to grey, then black.

33

a weed: un wanted plant
in mimicry of its surrounds

        bare-armed women
        sluice dead matter down drains

horsehair-broom bristles
affixed with horse glue

        an eye discerns
        one un like the others

grass grows above
iron, towards light

        even leaves
        have teeth

even leaves
have teeth

grass roots
regenerate blades

break in
crazed pattern

wild herds stampede
as wind rips at canvas

my mother's silken
hair an un bound river

under growth: persist
skywards; sun-memory

34

an orange dipper
bobs in a pail

river water runs off
husband's goosed skin

child's heart stops
and starts

father cradles a wooden
box of fruit

fingers part feathers
fire will take all

death in the afternoon
wild plants still flower

35

At the foot of the impossible stair
I finger the walls for a light

       Gauze grazes my skin

           Red: taut over wire
                 The steps go up and up

—If only I could ascend

       Emerge into the past
           Like clockwork undone

           Sheer balance

Tread there, and over here
       Dreams press their prints, disappear—

36

A child rises on all fours, wobbling. A child balances, arms
in the air, steadying the self. A child stumbles, over and over,
and we soothe the child. We know it is part of learning how
to walk: we fall, and we get up again. But not everyone
rises from the dead. Not every dead body becomes a tree,
or a flower.

37

I am six years old / I was born in November / I am in the
last class / My form teacher is Mrs Aw / I write with a
pencil / I do not know how to spell *orange* / how do you
say *zebra crossing* in Mandarin / I was caught thinking of
cheating on the test / I want to eat hot soup at recess time /
the bowl is red the noodles are yellow the fishballs are white
/ I don't like vegetables yet / the auntie cuts a hard-boiled
egg in half with a fishing line / it is like magic / I could
watch her all day long / when I grow up I will learn about
lots of things / a ring of green around the yolk means the
egg is overcooked / *Serious Eats* can be way too serious /
I once knew the names of all the moons of Jupiter / it seems
silly now to remember so much that is so useless / it is
true I am impatient with prose / there are many rules that
poetry can circumvent / I cannot pretend to understand
or make sense of everything that happens to me / anything
can happen in a poem like in a dream / but some poems
are nightmares / especially the rhyming ones / someone
you don't know chases you down a dark corridor / no end
in sight / da-DUM da-DUM da-DUM / you mustn't stop
running / your heart nearly explodes / I recently read a novel
I actually wanted to read / then I read another / they were
both very good although they were very different / by very
good I mean I wanted to keep on reading / the first gave me
a headache every time I picked it up / the mark of its genius
was how I kept hearing the voice in my head even after I'd
put the book down / writing is a kind of possession

38

some writers can animate your thoughts seemingly against
your will / though I suppose you could always just stop
reading / the second book I read was very quiet / all I could
think of was how the mother of the main character was so
unlike my own / if it had been my mother in the novel she
would have shouted nonstop / by which I mean her voice
would have been loud regardless of what she might have
been saying / I have heard my mother speak softly once or
twice / maybe she was at the tax office or at the hospital /
so I know she is capable of it / at least in theory / remember
you cannot talk at all during chapel or the teachers will
get you / but you are allowed to read the Bible in your lap
/ too bad it is quite boring / except for the sex bits / the
withdrawal method is unreliable unlike my maths grades /
nothing ever seems to add up / why do some people get to
write about other people then get upset when the people
they write about write back / ha-ha / it is about power of
course / my ex-therapist said it was obvious / no-one wants
to be told they are wrong / especially when they are wrong
/ it is far easier to double-down and dig in / sometimes a
poem is a window and sometimes a poem is a mirror and
sometimes a poem is a threshold and at all times poems are
lies / all writing is facsimile

39

a lot of art is about elevating the mundane because life is
mundane and people who are alive necessarily have to go
through the mundane again and again until they die / yes I
very much like the work of Do Ho Suh / the video reminds
me of that strange movie in which the characters had to jam
the lift between floors and force the doors open / did you
hear about the private after-hours party sponsored by some
big corporation / someone got drunk and fell through part
of the sculpture / the artist declined to comment / we do
not know if the artwork was insured / because of these rich
cunts I missed out on viewing the installation as it had been
intended by the artist / I wonder what it was like before the
museum removed the damaged sections / I guess I will never
know / oh wait you bought the catalogue / when we were
there in person I looked very carefully at the gauze and wire
replicas of bolts and hinges / light switches and wires / the
mechanisms of doorknobs / distinct components of the fire
extinguisher / remember the embroidered magna carta laid
out like a runner along the total length of the gallery once /
obviously not the same artist because you know / I spoke to
my friend about it / she said it was exploitative because they
used prison labour / 36 unnamed prisoners incarcerated
across 13 prisons did the bulk of the sewing / some famous
individuals stitched choice words like *freedom* and *liberty*
and *common people* / I was ashamed I had not realised that
grossness immediately

40

I read about how prisoners in Jinxiang are forced to peel
garlic cloves with their fingernails / until those crumble and
then they have to use their teeth / the smell leaves a trail
like an uncleared cache / rub your fingers over the back of
a stainless-steel spoon under running water / no real way
to remove the odour / Gao Rong I love her work / she was
born in Inner Mongolia / her family were from Shaanxi /
they were forced to relocate / they used to be landowners
you see / her grandmother traded craft for survival / seven
children raised on needle and thread / the billionaire must
have multiple hangars filled to the brim with this stuff /
I could not believe my eyes / her grandparents' home and
its contents reproduced in fine handiwork / floor tiles /
full-scale kang / flowered quilts / peeling paint / rusty
pipes / stove and wok / spatula and scoop / photographs in
frames / thermoses with peonies / a pair of enamel mugs /
washing machine and calendar and wall clock / mirrors and
windows and doors / each fibre a memory / an infinite spool
of remembrance / Do Ho Suh reconstructed his stove and
toilet and sink and pipes / a red stairway floating up to a
complete floor of somewhere other than here / his childhood
home encased in layers of mulberry paper and charcoal-
rubbed in its entirety / rubbing is a kind of loving / loving
is a method of living / poetry is a way to contain time /
writing is a type of fixity

41

artists recreate and reorder and replicate / the kitchen sink
with its padded dishes / fish bones sutured on an oval plate
/ triptych of the bus station sign / cash strings of cryptic
codes / unfired clay of the squat toilet / unfinished basin
and dripless tap / not all art is beautiful but truth can make
it so / find what you have to do / do it as well as you can
/ keep on doing it / for as long as is possible / our hands
press up against the glass / make your mark / bloodless
palms leave indecipherable smudges / we scroll past and
past / our mosaic of faces blur into one / you cut up many
flags / unpick new meanings from them / flowers are an
external manifestation of sex / details are parts of the whole
we cannot possibly fathom / it's nearly time / the laundry
basket is overflowing / the ironing pile must be gotten
through / you know you buy less when you shop on foot
without a trolley / but my hands hurt from carrying the
bags / remember I broke my foot recently / no poems have
been accepted this week / someone dropped out of the
session so you could attend for free / who would pay to
talk about white privilege to a roomful of whites / Chinese
waiters serve us Chinese food / no-one eats the roast duck
leg because it would be too messy / would anyone notice
if I wrapped it in a napkin and put it in my bag for later /
what goes around doesn't always come around / karma is a
chameleon / I push the glistening drumstick away on the
lazy susan / bye-bye / bye // bye

42

I sift through old photographs. Here is a man who clutched wooden blocks that he shuffled and clapped in the dirt in order to move forward, to live. A taxonomy of heights: some must be above, and so others must stay below. My ancestors trained their eyes on the ground they tilled, watching the feet of those who would crush them without a care. Their carcasses: a runway for those who would take flight. The sky beyond reach for them, and for me.

43

And yet we have eyes, we have hands, have feet, have bodies, minds, histories, futures. We, too, are present. Who watches whom? Do we ever stop performing? You who watch us, you who do not care what happens behind the curtain, even as you mouth the same lines blurred by so many tongues before yours. Words so brittle they crumble into meaningless noise.

44

I sit opposite you. You like the sun on your skin, but
I remain in the shadows. I watch your mouth open and
close, close and open. I hear you, but I am not listening.
I am in the kitchen where my grandmother fillets the fish
my grandfather caught on a line. She makes her cuts, grasps
the edge of fish-skin firmly, and tears it away in one smooth
motion. There are so many fish left to catch, to salt against
the famine to come.

45

Still afternoons traversing
splintered hills and caves on display.

Eighteen immortals, hollowed faces distinct.
Protruding ribs of one so close to nirvana.

Lift the dome, and the scent of rosewood—
resinous, faintly floral—rises above

nicotine and smoke, leather and sulphur.
Traced letters in an unfamiliar language.

Mother-of-pearl chrysanthemums inlaid
on benches, chairs, tables: offerings

from men he'd cared for, had brought to the new
country. Incense thins, dissipates with wind.

46

In my dream, I was sitting in my usual seat
at the round table in my grandmother's kitchen.

Next to it, the living room—a wooden bench
where the sofa should have been, carved

with flowers inlaid with bright mother-of-pearl:
a partial repayment of a debt owed to my dead

grandfather. Also accepted: sandalwood sculptures
of eighteen luohan in glass cases, their expressions

grotesque in eternal speechlessness. The crags
of the mountains where the immortals perched

were wet with our tears. We learned not only
of his death, but of our own fates: to become moths

hurling our small bodies over and over at backlit
doors that would never open for us.

In my dream, my grandmother was serving me
steamed dumplings in a rice bowl.

I picked one up with chopsticks and bit it
in half. It was filled with words; they oozed

across blue-and-white porcelain. There were
Chinese characters and letters from the English

alphabet. I coughed up confetti into a pink
napkin; golden numerals spilled from the cloth

onto the tiled floor. I asked for some tea. My grandmother
reached into the wicker basket, and lifted out a grey rock

with a spout and a handle. Little red fish swam in my cup,
but when I raised it to my lips, they burst into yellow

starfish that unfurled like suns. I knew it was only a dream
because I was in my bed, alone. I was far from her, and home.

47

It was like this: I thought I was in love. I said to myself:
This is what love is. I saw it happen to others. I did not think
happiness was compatible with my reality. I understood
only the characters for doorway, table, and bed. I thought
marriage was an envelope into which I could seal the secret
poetry of myself. I left it dormant in a drawer until one day,
when I found a dull knife. I honed its edge on the underside
of a china bowl, the way my grandmother had taught me.

48

We return to the room at the top
of the stairs with a strip of windows
along one wall. Floorboards splinter

underfoot. A bed, a cradle, and, one night,
a rat—it gnaws on the child's foot, blood
soaking the sheets before he wakes, crying.

49

From the fourth-storey window,
a girl watches her brother emerge
from within the block of flats

and make his way uphill along
the path, jangling a pocketful of coins.
The trees obscure her view, and he is gone.

50

I stood in the bright kitchen
and ironed a shirt at midnight.
He laughed at me, and called me naïve.

I heard the man in the next apartment
cough without stopping. His wife switched on the light.
The pipes in the wall shuddered when she ran the taps.

51

The children searched for the skeletons
of leaves in dead matter. They stained
them with dye then sealed them in plastic.

Years later, she found one pressed between
the pages of a book. Through the painted lace
she read these words: *fire, stillness, ashes.*

52

In the dresser drawer, beneath
his jumpers, he kept a collection
of knives. The largest was serrated.

Before she left, she dropped the blades
down the rubbish chute, one after the other:
like letters without addresses, without stamps.

53

The day you left, I knew I would not
see you again. Your mother and father
were waiting, and your lover was watching

from the other side of the world. All those times
we'd pledged our loyalty and pressed our pens together,
I wondered when and how it would fall apart.

54

In a room at the end of the corridor
evening descends beyond the windows.
We round the corner; the patient is slack-jawed

but breathing. Difficult to believe she once danced
and sang. She laughs in a photograph, aged three.
We draw the blanket over her chest, and leave.

55

Each night we slough off our old selves
in our sleep. I dream of buses, of untethered
balloons. Every night I try to stay intact.

The bed is a grave; the sheets, a shroud.
In the morning you raise the blinds, and I wake.
I remember all things. I understand nothing.

56

Traffic sounds rising through
the window of the bedroom.

The old man pushes his cart
along the road. Bright brooms

and buckets, a wonderland
of household apparatus.

Great-grandmother buys
a bundle of sticks for scrubbing

out the wok, pulling out a note
from within her blouse. The rain

drums on the tin roof of the kitchen;
enamel basins become little ponds.

57

We throw out peelings into the drains,
the smell of rotting vegetables thick

in the heat. In the cool, tiled bathroom
cockroaches dart across blue and green.

Outside, the kettle is whistling
on the stove, so loud the bowls

shiver in the cabinet. The cats slip
into the room through the bars

of the window. They see him touch me.
I understand nothing. I remember everything.

58

I was just twelve. I stood in a crowd with a crucifix tied around my neck. I looked up and saw him: blue-eyed, impossibly blond. The mirrors stared back. Between the covers of the books I read: only white girls. What language had I inherited? What languages have I lost? In the museums, long-dead animals are stuffed and posed, forever hunted and dying.

59

we speak words so tiny they cluster
on the back of a solitary horse lengthening

when the moonlight lays its soft whip
over the knot underpinned by a heart

into which a sword carves its long lines
under the roof of the shell we carry

hand-pulled dough thrown across a slab
doubling in volume given time and more time

a wide belt ribboned around the narrow hips
of my name-sister cooking hotpot in a cold room

on the other side of the world while she dreams
smoothly in a language I lost my tongue stretched

like scalded rain falling within clouds over hours
we cannot add up because we ran out of tape

with this bowl we put off hunger for one more day

60

The roast in the oven grown cold
The empty bed

Her hair on your coat
No letters for weeks

Rain all day
The garden near drowned

The lost cat
Its collar worn through

61

A broken glass
Wine on the carpet

The mirror last night
Pages of a book

I build a fire
Your handwriting collapses

The gate fallen off its hinges
A rusted latch

62

The sky / full of omens

      blood and fur on the driveway

two birds landed on a bare branch, claws locking

      the wind picked up / died down

in the dark the water is indistinguishable from night

      look! a fox on the sand—

63

rusty carcass of a car collapsed by the roadside

      they made us walk through the fields seeded with landmines

we crush weevils / cook them with rice

      a soldier with a gun arrested a ten-year-old boy, rocks at his feet

a woman dragged across the square, her blouse torn open

      a dream takes root in a crack / a tree cleaves a stone in two

64

screen spits into life. wasteland:
ochre dust, unbreathable sky. dying sun.

helicopters throb above blown trees. lights
flash blue-red, police lock innocents in homes.

today, a bomb—shells of buildings, of homes.
rubble, rock. blood, bodies. a child's thin cries.

draw breath and exhale. cloud of moisture
condenses. remove your face; discard it in the soil.

in the mornings, there is still a harbour. the man
who shares your bed is half asleep. you kiss—

65

streets full of people who touch everything,
and one another. they cough, they laugh aloud.

the river divides the old town. spirit
flows along bedrock, carries mist gospel.

we fold the gilded papers carefully. today, we are
making cranes. count to a thousand, then release them.

in the meadow by the salt sea, plovers arc overhead.
they stutter warnings. we find and break all their eggs.

veiled moon: black shapes flit across her fullness.
the closer we move to the mystery, the less we see—

66

My mother blew air into arm floats and pulled first my hands then my arms through the tight openings. The sharp seams scratched my skin, leaving long red welts. All she wanted was for me to survive. I was an insect in a lake, struggling to stay on the surface. My legs pointed down towards the depths, threshing. Those who try to drown me do not realise that there are beings whose entire lives exist underwater, for whom breath is liquid weight.

67

At three, I learned how to bite to draw blood without breaking skin.
I was once a giant cat for whom trees were splinters and lakes, footbaths.
At ten, I set fire to a paper house so my grandfather could live in luxury.

Oysters speak in riddles and spit at one another out of love and desire.
We collected dull brown shells from kelp, knowing they were rainbows.
I swam for seven days and seven nights before I entered the kingdom of coral and pearls.

I have never once wept out of anger or fear.
Nothing anyone says about me can hurt me any longer.
I do not retain anything I write for fear it might all come true.

68

We are the blinking human cargo, transported in the sunless hold, as the deck opens to the day. New arrivals in an unknown land. Knowledge, the first mapping; mapping, the first act of possession. To define in language, in marks on a page. But what of the ones we do not write of, who refuse to be contained in vessels of our own making? Some truths cannot be compressed into words, onto paper.

69

my ancestors squint towards dry land from the deck
of a ship, or are they like swine, packed into the hull
to see the sun only when they arrive for the slaughter

how do you tell those who have survived
it is better to die than to live by trampling
on the throats of others or we are no better than

the masters who crack the whips; some of us
bend and some of us break and still some dream
at night of wielding weapons so they too may rise

but to what end: a long line to stand in and feed on
the lie that we will be next, possessing nothing but scrawl
of dragon and phoenix on rice paper devoured by flame

70

Grit enters an oyster. The mollusc tries to eject the invader.
If it fails at its task, it begins to coat the foreign object with
its own secretions, layer by layer, to soften the edges, to take
the hurt away. People harvest the shells and prise them open,
greedy for pearls. They trade gleaming strands for land,
for slaves. They learn how to seed flesh. They farm pain.
Each pearl as beautiful and useless as the death that haunts it:
bleached like teeth, like bones.

71

The gate is locked. A woman
leaves the house, and we enter.
My grandmother takes her seat
at the table. Her braceleted arms
cross others as they churn the tiles:
dry seas breaking over papered felt.

72

She pulls a tile and runs her thumb
along its underside, over its carved
indentations. In a single swift motion,
she discards it. Her eyes search for the key.
When it comes to her, her fingers insert
the tile into the gap. She calls *pung!* and wins.

73

The week my grandfather dies, my grandmother
gives up mahjong for a year. All are bereft:
an empty space, a missing place. She lies in bed,
unsleeping, hearing his voice in every room.
Four decades of arguments, six children, nine
grandchildren—a pyre, ashes, and a memorial.

74

I watched as my grandmother rose from her bed
and went to the bathroom without closing the door.
Lately, she has taken to stripping off and wandering
the apartment, naked. One day, she remembers my name.
The next, she speaks only of the dead. Nearly endgame.
Her final round—the clacking of the cold jade tiles.

75

I cradled the legs of a raw chicken in my hands
and thought: *this is dead flesh.* It was my grandfather

who ate the first meal I ever prepared. He died
that same year. The morning after my grandmother

passed on, my mother asked for rice porridge.
It is palatable comfort; we are bereft, and crippled.

On screen, my grandmother's eyes were dulled.
My voice rang out in the room: empty echoes.

76

When I was seven, and hungry, I'd asked her
to cook me lunch from a packet of instant congee.

I read the instructions out loud, counted down
the minutes, and said it was ready. She showed me

the rice grains: still hard, and unyielding. *I can't
find my way to the other side*, she'd cried. *Do not shake*

my body when I am gone, or my soul will scatter—I hold
no vigil by her coffin. I burn only joss-paper words.

77

On the forty-ninth day, I dreamed of you. We sat on the
shores of a lake, lying back on lounges. I wanted to look
at your face, at you, but my eyes only saw two folding fans
nestled in the damp grass. The fan on the left was painted
gold, and the other, a glossy black—a pair of snakes at rest.
The surface of the lake scintillated with a strange half-light.
Both of us suspended in time: not-living, undying. I was
startled by a sound not of my making—the lake became a
bed, and my dream surfaced into morning. The snakes' soft
gullets yawned soundlessly, and I swallowed.

78

Remember when I used to cry?

And how, one day, you cut up a chilli
and rubbed it in my eyes?

You laugh—

You say, *I thought I'd give you
something to cry about.*

I remember. And you did.

79

I draw a map. I shade the blue in, and label all the elements. I take particular care with the stones. They have been worn down by moving water, which is also the hand of time. Each pebble has its own distinct heaviness; they have been shaped and shaped again. The river is wide and slow-moving here. See how it branches out into many tributaries, until the land cannot hold itself against the water, and spills into sea. This is the delta. The mouth of the river only a memory. All that begins ends, and begins again.

80

it was a walled city—here the crumbling
fortifications and towers flanking
the gates. an entryway cut into one side
of the giant doors, metal-studded, hung
on enormous hinges. brackets held metal
bolts ten men found impossible to shift.

>the inscriptions: roman numerals add up to
>decades, centuries. latin buried in the mouth, roots
>obscured, running in veins. paved roads and plazas,
>basilicas and cathedrals. naves, alcoves, statues, tomb-
>stones. domes and rotundas. a well, a dried-up echo.

trees in hushed rows, heat shimmering
from exposed ground. no grass in between.
the oranges are growing in the grove. women
wearing aprons hand-pick globes and slowly
stack them in baskets. machines are ruthless.
fruit harvested before ripeness will still bruise.

81

Nearly winter. The farmer and his wife go out
among the trees to harvest the olives. They stack
branches for burning, bag black fruit into sacks, then
pile them high by the stony walls. Tomorrow, their sons
will take the harvest to sell at the market in the old town.

It is night, and the farmer watches over his fields.
There are wild boars about. They are hungry. The farmer
has no working rifle, and the beasts are unafraid of stones.
His dogs bark at the darkness. The cats watch and do nothing.
His wife calls out to him, and slowly he returns to the hut.

82

The farmer and his wife lie side by side in their bed.
They each think of the other's death. They do not speak of it.
In the morning, they work flour, salt and water into dough, shape it
into loaves, and light the fire for the oven. They pull warm bread
apart, dip it in oil and eat it under the trees with their neighbours.

One spring morning, the farmer gathers his basket of tools
and leaves the hut for the fields. He does not return at noon;
his lunch is left uneaten. They find him after sunset, lying
in the newly ploughed earth, eyes open, one hand on his heart,
the other full of seeds. His wife palms the hollow of his chest.

83

We walk, unhurried, in the manicured gardens. You look
unwell. I understand why—you have travelled to the
underside of the world only to come face to face with your
own history. How do I tell you we cannot escape? There are
no straight lines away from our origins. In the middle of this
plotted wilderness, there is a temple built without a single
nail. Inside it, incense-spirals burn. Sweet smoke rises to the
dovetailed rafters and permeates the wood.

84

I once read a book of love poems written
by someone who was part-lizard. Another, part-
snake, writhed in the tall grass. I ran, unseeing,

pushing through the uncut lalang. There was no secret
trampled path of safety where others had fled before.
When I finally emerged from the field, my dress was

in ribbons. Those watching could no longer read
the truth. Rubies melted into pomegranate
seeds within a coffin; cakes crumbled in our mouths.

A thin facsimile of pipes reeded through the sound system.
We sat directly under the air-conditioning vent. Our tears
froze like perfect chandeliers. They fell and shattered across

the black-and-white tiles. I'd made myself a rose but pinned
it upside down. They lost an amethyst in the green plastic grass
but it was me who found it under a torn paper cup. I know magic.

85

The spinning wheels glow neon-green. Water released
from the mouth of the dam roars over the bolted
edge into the reservoir. We mine energy: disconnect
from the pod and emerge, newborn and knowing. Time
hurtles down dimly lit corridors, a cat's ears rotate
unthinkingly to the origin of sound. Strings of copper cash
now worthless. People rush to exchange them for trays
of rotting persimmons. Melt metal in the furnace, cast copper
into a series of hanging bells. The king struck one: its thin
reverberations blurred the air, travelled up his arm into his body
and stopped his heart. A mountain woman sings songs
of her ancestors into the mouthpiece of a computer
held in one hand. We hear music, and coloured bulbs
light up in tandem. A white man stalks a black crowd;
he collects their cadences for an ivory grave. Telegraph wires
divide whole forests; they cannot bear our human weight.

86

The ceiling slopes upwards, and back down again. A globe, round and white as the moon, is suspended overhead. Four faceless musicians are on stage; another is hidden behind the gleaming piano. Lamplight and shadows. Glasses clink, and voices murmur. The room is warm and smoky. Time is of no consequence here. Off-canvas, a barman polishes a wooden counter, over and over. Someone leaves the club; the door swings open and shut, shut and open.

87

Twelve people lie on beanbags in a darkened room, facing a wide, bright screen. In every projected frame, there is a clock face visible—on a wrist, a mantelpiece, a tower in the distance. The audience is silent and suspended. Occasionally, a watcher might wonder what time it is on the outside. People get up and leave. Others enter and take their place. Time is ever-present, ticking by, minute by synchronised minute.

88

The blade of the sword cut so swiftly and with such precision that it barely left a mark. The blood told another story: bloomed flowers clung at skin, spread throughout the bedclothes, soaked into the woven mats. It is said that the lovers had lingered in the room at the inn for days on end, refusing food and water, devouring only each other, until their appetites could no longer be sated, even as they shuddered unto their deaths.

89

Two hundred people sit in a theatre. The lights have been dimmed; the stage is spotlit. The filmmaker is speaking: no copies exist save for the original print in the room. The film is sent across countries, it passes through hands, through the machine; it deteriorates with every screening. One day, it will simply fall apart and cease to exist. Every single person who appears in the movie is dead, even as they eat, drink, and breathe out great clouds of smoke. No-one else seems to know or care that it is the seventh lunar month, or that we are all already ghosts, shuffling towards the final flickering sign.

90

The stench of death is its own sickly perfume. First it was birds, then rodents, then the cold, stiffening body of the cat itself. When the heart stops beating, blood in the veins stills, and the body begins to consume itself. Bruises bloom under the skin, the body bloats then decomposes into fluid. Someone holds a skull up to the sun; worms feed on what we can no longer see, digesting death into their wriggling, glistening selves. Listen—you can hear their jaws opening and closing—they are, in fact, singing.

91

I am tired of running. My earliest memory is that of being carried while my mother ran, the world blurring by. What do we run from? Stones cut our feet so deeply that the roads we have followed are stained red by our blood. My mother shows me a scan and points to a shadow where a hole has opened up in the left chamber of her heart. Perhaps it has always been there. I pray her heart keeps beating. Whole forests are watered by our sweat, our tears.

92

Every step we took
echoed in the hills.
Clouds dispersed
by gusts of north wind.

Beyond the ridge, mists
descended over
the old poet's dreams
of rice wine, of moonlight.

93

We never uttered
a single cry. We
bent our heads across
our laps; we stitched

what visions arrived.
Outside, chickens
scrabbled at bare dirt;
grew stringy, hungrier.

94

Willows droop with rain
on autumn evenings.
We beat wet cloth on rocks
that line the riverbanks.

Streams swell; water will
rise and wash away
this ink. Begin again,
forget all past words.

95

On the slopes, the girls
sing so sweetly, like
the herbs they gather
for the old poet's

tinctures. We light the
hearth, recite verses till
embers die. Only then
may we fall asleep.

96

Who do we wait for?
No-one sings mountain
songs anymore. Girls
grown into women

who leave the hills
for distant cities.
The only sounds left:
wind, river, static.

97

We go to my parents' home for dinner
once a week when we are in the same country.

They want us to live with them, the way
they did with their parents in the other country.

Sorry, I'm not that sort of Asian, I tell them.
I'm not like my friends in the old country,

where grandparents are carers for grandchildren,
and parents leave to work in distant countries.

98

I think of the men who first came to Australia,
sold as coolie labour to the new country.

How they survived amid squalor. Some farmed
vegetables in thin soil on mining country.

In the old museum, a tattered, handmade flag—
ROLL UP! ROLL UP! No Chinese in gold country!

Brittle clippings: in 1928, a woman bearing my name
arrived as a young bride from her father's country.

She was detained, then arrested and deported,
even though she had been born in this country.

99

My parents pack their suitcases and leave
to return to the un/familiar country.

Their parents are now dead. Our families'
graves: scattered across so many countries.

I buy funeral goods from overseas for my ancestors.
No-one makes them in this faraway country.

I fold silver ingots from coarse joss paper, a skill
my fingers honed at vigils in my home country.

100

At night I wander our shophouse, long since
demolished. It exists only in dream country.

I burn my offerings. All turns to ash. Can spirits
find their descendants lost in foreign countries?

How do you put down roots in stolen country?
I thirst. The earth is salt. I am alone in every country.

101

And what did you leave me
in the end?

A mouthful
of fish and rice chewed to a paste:
don't run, eat more, grow strong.

Pineapples for the ancestral altar
crafted from blank lottery forms.

At your friend's home,
in a room converted into a salon:
the shorter the better, you use less shampoo.

Breaking tails off beansprouts,
removing heads of dried anchovies.

Never once read me a book:
too late for me, but not too late for you.
Taught me to make tea, to cook, to sew.

Survived your childhood, the war,
motherhood, your marriage.

Braced me when I left:
not good to you, good to me for what?
Our feet were the exact same size.

In the beginning, there was you.
No end: to this grief, to our love.

Notes

The first epigraph is an excerpt from Li-Young Lee's 'Furious Versions' from *The City in Which I Love You*. Copyright © 1990 by Li-Young Lee. Reprinted with the permission of The Permissions Company, LLC on behalf of BOA Editions, Ltd., boaeditions.org. The second epigraph is from Emily Dickinson's 'Bloom—is Result—to meet a Flower', public domain, last accessed at The Adrian Brinkerhoff Poetry Foundation's website <www.brinkerhoffpoetry.org/poems/bloom-is-result-to-meet-a-flower> on 6 October 2023.

In fragment 16, 'Almásy' refers to Count Ladislaus de Almásy, the titular character of Michael Ondaatje's novel *The English Patient* (1992, McClelland and Stewart, Toronto, Ontario). The quote, however, is not from the novel but from the screenplay of the adaptation by Anthony Minghella (1995), reprinted with permission from The Saul Zaentz Company, Berkeley, California, USA.

Fragment 59 is a response to the Chinese character *biáng*, as in *biángbiángmiàn*, the handmade noodles that originate from Xi'an in Shaanxi province. At 58 strokes, the onomatopoeic *biáng* is the most complex character in the Chinese language and, while commonly used, is not included in any dictionaries.

Fragments 60 and 61 owe a debt to Dalya Alberge's article 'Sex, Lies and Despair: Unseen letters reveal Larkin's tortured love', published in *The Guardian* on 24 May 2020, last accessed at <www.theguardian.com/books/2020/

may/24/sex-lies-and-despair-unseen-letters-reveal-larkins-tortured-love> on 21 November 2023.

Some fragments are responses to artworks, TV series and films, including: Frida Kahlo's *What the Water Gave Me* (1938); Lee Isaac Chung's *Minari* (2020); Do Ho Suh's *My Home/s (Vertical) (2014–2019)*, the *Hub* series, in particular *Hub: Unit G5, Union Wharf, 23 Wenlock Road, London N1 7SB, UK* (2015), *Stove, Apartment A, 348 West 22nd Street, New York, NY 10011, USA* (2013), *Toilet, Apartment A, 348 West 22nd Street, New York, NY 10011, USA* (2013), *Basin, Apartment A, 348 West 22nd Street, New York, NY 10011, USA* (2015), *Staircase III* (2010), *Rubbing/Loving Project: Seoul Home* (2013–2022), *Floor* (1997–2000), and *Who Am We? (Multicoloured)* (2000); Spike Jonze and Charlie Kaufman's *Being John Malkovich* (1999); Cornelia Parker's *Magna Carta: An Embroidery* (2015); Gao Rong's *The Static Eternity* (2012), *Level 1/2, Unit 8, Building 5, Hua Jiadi, North Village* (2010), *Station* (2011), and *Some Days Later* (2015); Lin Zhi's *Afraid of Water* (2013); Raquel Ormella's *Australia Rising #2* (2009), *New Constellation #1* (2013) and *Wealth for Toil #1* (2014); Robert Rauschenberg's *This Is a Portrait of Iris Clert If I Say So* (1961); Liu Chuang's *Bitcoin Mining and Field Recordings of Ethnic Minorities* (2018); Diana Lim's *Untitled* (2016); Christian Marclay's *The Clock* (2010); Nagisa Oshima's *In the Realm of the Senses* (1976); Charlie Shackleton's *The Afterlight* (2021); and Kim Jin-woo's *A Model Family* (2022).

Acknowledgements

We Speak of Flowers was written on the unceded Gadigal land of the Eora Nation. I pay my respects to all Aboriginal Elders past and present.

I also wish to express my gratitude for the care shown to me and this project by various people over the years.

Thank you to my friend and colleague Lisa Gorton for her careful, thoughtful editing of the manuscript, and for believing in this book. To my publisher UQP, especially Aviva Tuffield for her continued support, Felicity Dunning for her keen editorial eye, and Madeline Byrne for the stunning cover design.

To my brother, the artist Heman Chong, for acceding to my request for an artwork for the cover of this book, and for creating a piece so unsettlingly apt and unique.

To my parents, John and Diana, for their unwavering love, support and sympathy at my chosen profession, and my grandparents, who loved me beyond measure.

To my mentors who I am privileged to also call friends: Judith Beveridge, Joanne Burns and Boey Kim Cheng, for their guidance, encouragement and ongoing devotion to our beloved craft.

Thank you to Eda Gunaydin, Roanna Gonsalves, Jenna Guillaume, Sara Saleh, Eunice Andrada, Sarah Stivens,

Panda Wong, Elizabeth Allen, Lachlan Brown, Judith
Bishop, Felicity Plunkett, Marieke Hardy, Michael Bradley
and Thomas Keneally for their vital, writerly friendship
and support.

To esteemed poets Alison Whittaker, Bella Li and
Andy Jackson for their kind words on the book.

To the artist Raquel Ormella, for her generous friendship
and beautiful artworks.

To my childhood friends Pamela C.W.L., Janice L., Joanne L.,
Cheryl T., Pamela C. and Kelvin C. for their steady love and
care over the decades.

To our friends Marshall H., Elliott M., Sonal P., Piotr P.,
Alison R., Matthew P., Tegan W., Andrew M., and my
Australian cousins J.P., J.C., J.J., C.N. and J.G., thank you
for imbuing my days with love, meaning and connection.

To all the students and teachers I have worked with over the
years, thank you for keeping the flame of poetry alive in me
while also supporting my writing through paid employment.

And most of all, to my husband, Colin, a beacon of love,
care, good humour and unfaltering faith in me.

Sections of this book were variously published as individual
poems in slightly different forms. My sincere thanks to the
editors of the following journals for taking my work:
*The Australian, Australian Book Review, Best of Australian
Poems 2022, Best of Australian Poems 2023, Best of Australian*

Poems 2024, Cordite Poetry Review, Going Down Swinging, Griffith Review, Island, Kalliope X, the lickety-split, Magma Poetry, Meanjin, Newcastle Poetry Prize Anthology 2021, Newcastle Poetry Prize Anthology 2023, Overland, Portside Review, QWERTY, Rabbit, The Saturday Paper, Sine Theta Magazine, Southerly, The Suburban Review, Wasafiri and *Writing NSW.*

Fragments of the book were commissioned by the University of Canberra for *Poetry on the Move* in 2020, by Correspondences for *Thinking of Immortality & Kindness* in 2020, by The Story Factory for *In A Flash* in 2022, and by *Liminal Review of Books* for *Synthesis* in 2023 (edited by Eda Gunaydin).

Several fragments of the book (as individual poems) were longlisted for the Peter Porter Poetry Prize 2021, were highly commended in the Newcastle Poetry Prize 2021 and were shortlisted for the Newcastle Poetry Prize 2023.

Several fragments of the book (as individual poems) were published in the chapbook *Notes on Tomb-Sweeping* (Gazebo Books, 2024).

This project has been assisted by the Australian Government through the Australia Council, its arts funding and advisory body, and also by the NSW Government through Create NSW, its arts funding and advisory body.

A THOUSAND CRIMSON BLOOMS
Eileen Chong

I dreamed everyone, even my own
mother, had forgotten my name—

Eileen Chong's luminous poetry examines the histories—personal, familial and cultural—that form our identities and obsessions. *A Thousand Crimson Blooms* is a deepening of her commitment to a poetics of sensuous simplicity and complex emotions, even as she confronts the challenges of infertility or fraught mother–daughter relations. Entwined throughout are questions of migration and belonging. Viewed as a whole, this collection is a field of flowers, aflame with light.

'*A Thousand Crimson Blooms* is Eileen Chong's most powerful collection yet. The word "courage" rings through these poems.'
Lisa Gorton

'These are sustaining, necessary poems for our desperate times. Their uncompromising honesty and beauty question, confront, praise, uplift and celebrate human life in all its bewildering complexity.' **Boey Kim Cheng**

'Spare in form though rich in language, gesture and signification, this new collection extends Eileen Chong's range and accomplishment.' **Paul Kane**

ISBN 978 0 7022 6319 4

www.ingramcontent.com/pod-product-compliance
Ingram Content Group UK Ltd.
Pitfield, Milton Keynes, MK11 3LW, UK
UKHW030931050225
454656UK00004B/139